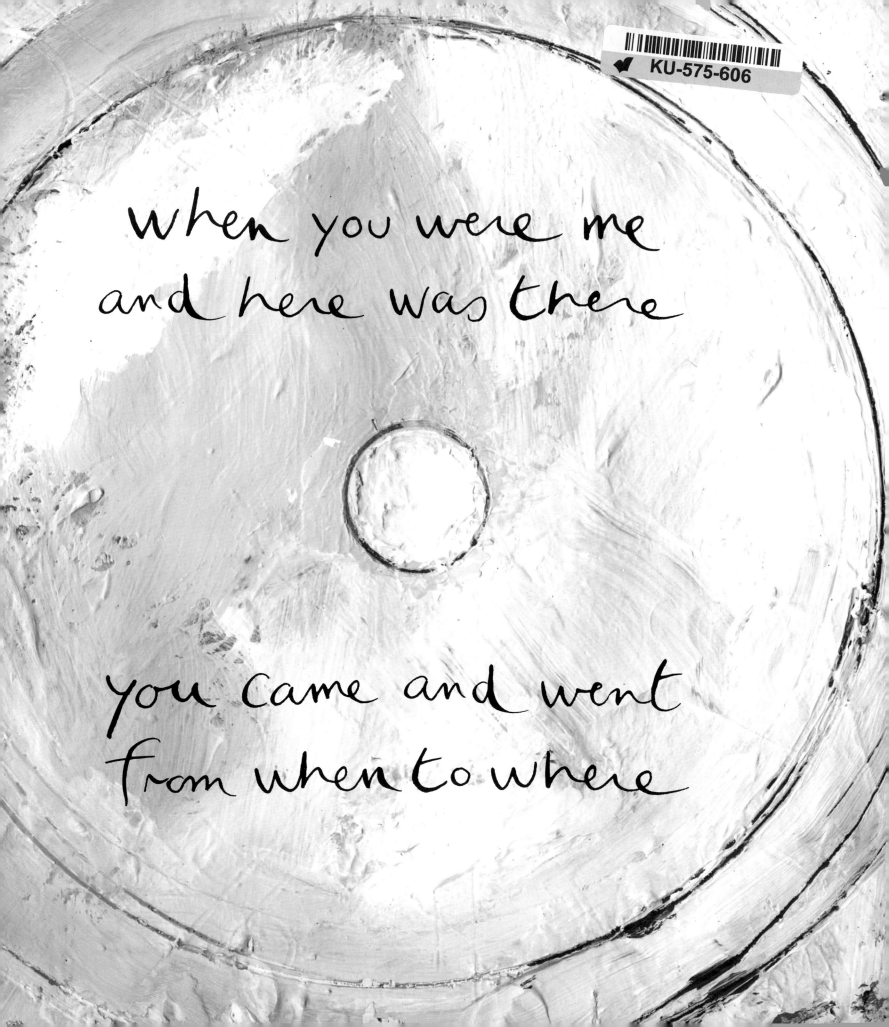

You found a place
where I wasn't me

You shut your eyes
and you could see...

An
Apple
All Alone

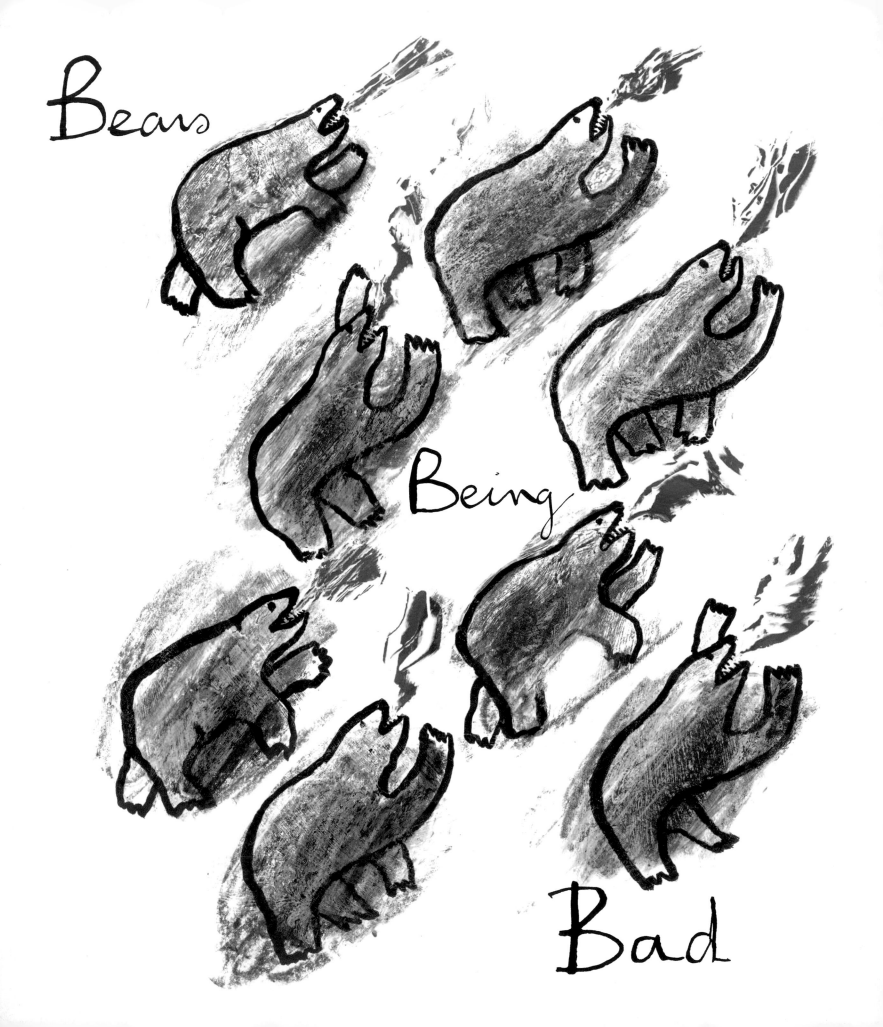

dogs drawing dad

it was where...

ICE CREAM is itchy

Kittens

Kick
Ketchup

lipstick

leans

Noses
Need
Nets

OWLS OPEN OVENS

people

polish

pets

UNICORNS UPSET VISITING VET

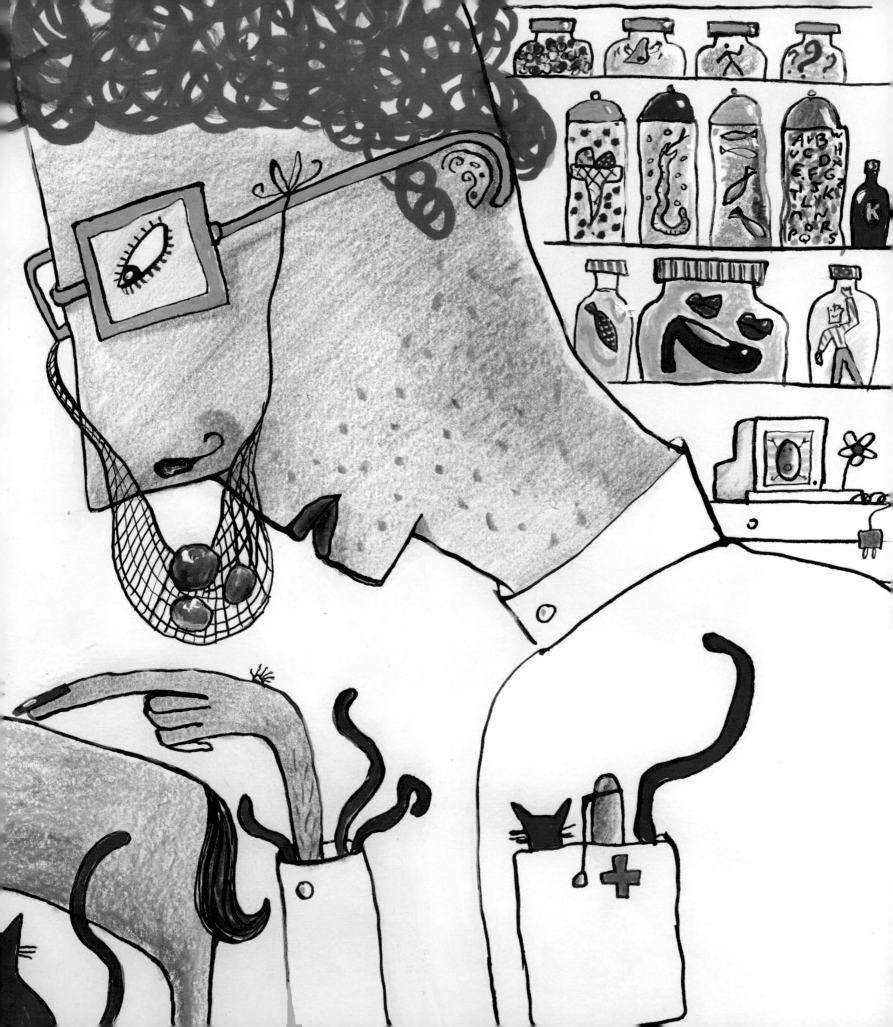

ZEBRA.

ZOO!